D1552163

BUG

GOES THROUGH THE

MAZE

WRITTEN & ILLUSTRATED BY

K. M. GROSHEK

BUG'S ADVENTURE SERIES

Disclaimer: This book is an artistic work of creative expression and is not an advertisement for or endorsement of any products or services. This book, content and characters are not affiliated with, endorsed by, nor associated with any automobile company or any other manufacture of automotive products or services.

Copyright © K.M. Groshek 2010. All Rights Reserved. No part of this book may be reproduced or transmitted in any form or by any means, graphic, electronic, or mechanical, including photocopying, recording, taping, or by any information storage retrieval system, without the permission, in writing, from the publisher.

Printed in the United States by BookMasters, Inc., 30 Amberwood Parkway, Ashland, OH 44805 M7159, April 2010

ISBN 978-0-9843521-4-2

Published by Creatively Canny Madison, WI 53719 www.creativelycanny.com

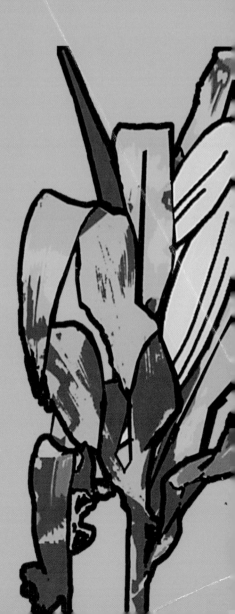

For my family and friends.

— K.M. Groshek

A bright yellow bug
went down the long road;
when he came to a cornfield,
he took notice and slowed.

Bug realized he passed
this way every day;
it was time to explore it,
if he could find the right way.

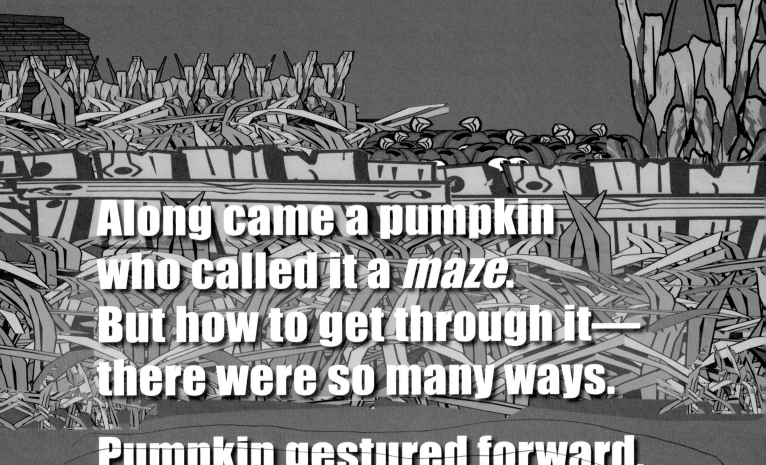

Along came a pumpkin
who called it a *maze*.
But how to get through it—
there were so many ways.

Pumpkin gestured forward,
"It's time now to start!"
Bug felt rather nervous,
with a twinge in his heart.

5

6

Bug screwed up his courage
and ventured forth to the light;
Shimmering corn went for miles
till all out of sight.

Then Bug saw a flower
who shared quite a lot:
"Yes, this is a maze,
but a labyrinth it's not."

8

"A labyrinth is simple,
it goes to the center and back;
But a maze is a puzzle;
it takes thinking and knack.

Take your time and enjoy
every path and new sight;
The choices are endless,"
she began to recite.

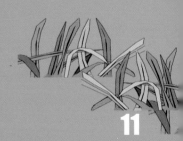

Bug nodded, quite thankful
and went down the road,
Realizing quickly,
a choice would unfold.

Then suddenly before him,
a path split in two,
He felt so confused,
asking, *What should I do?*

13

Waiting a moment
till he could decide,
He reviewed some ideas
before picking one side.

Cautiously striding
the path that he chose,
Heading, quite carefully,
down the corn rows.

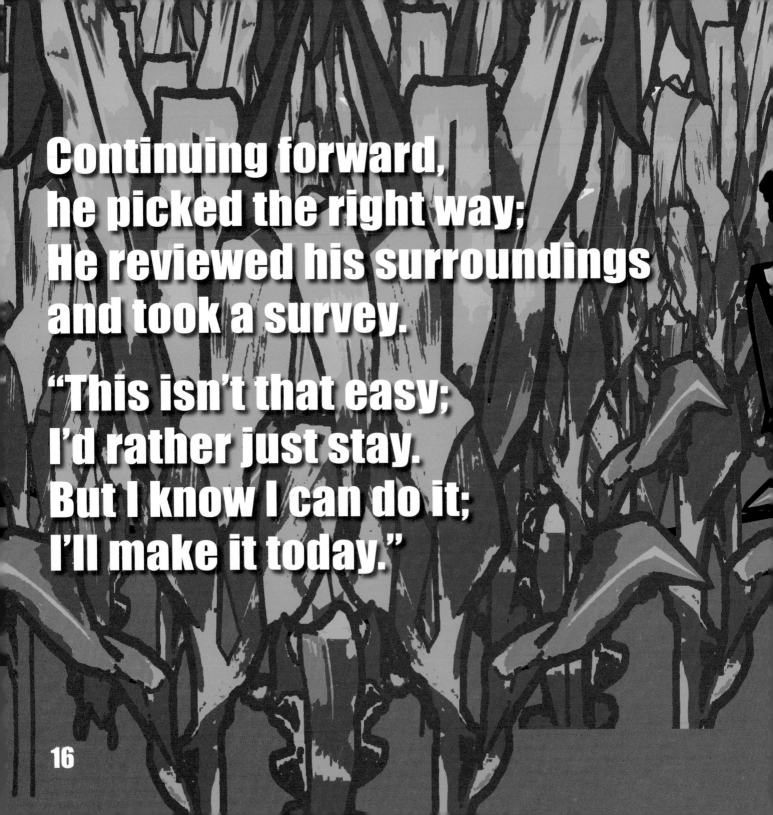

Continuing forward,
he picked the right way;
He reviewed his surroundings
and took a survey.

"This isn't that easy;
I'd rather just stay.
But I know I can do it;
I'll make it today."

Bug soon reached a clearing
within one corn row;
Then out popped from nowhere,
a frantic scarecrow.

The scarecrow seemed burdened;
Bug asked him, "What's wrong?"
Scarecrow squeaked just a little,
his voice was not strong.

19

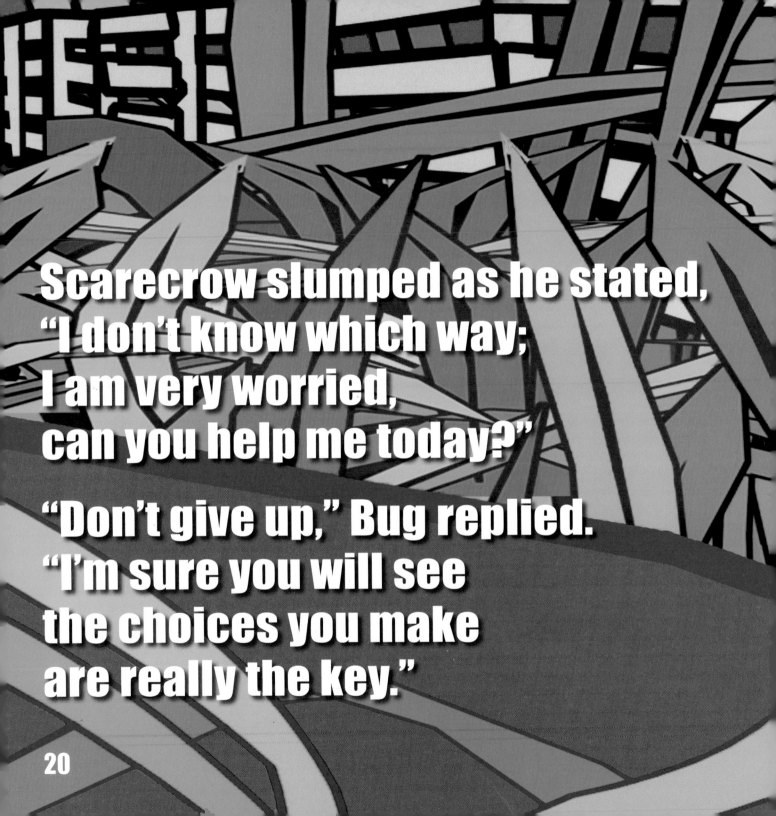

Scarecrow slumped as he stated,
"I don't know which way;
I am very worried,
can you help me today?"

"Don't give up," Bug replied.
"I'm sure you will see
the choices you make
are really the key."

21

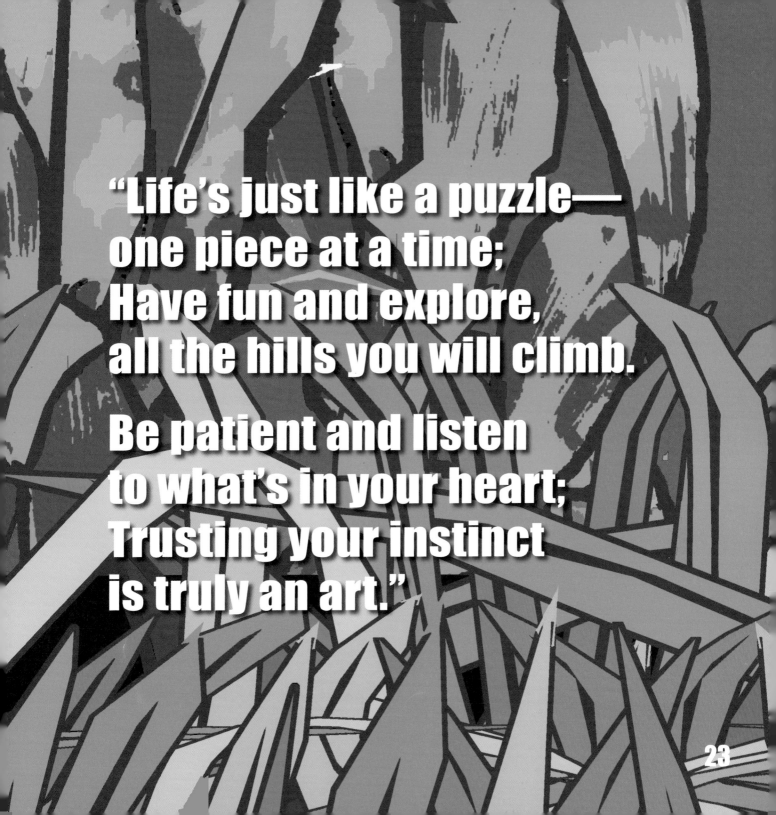

"Life's just like a puzzle—
one piece at a time;
Have fun and explore,
all the hills you will climb.

Be patient and listen
to what's in your heart;
Trusting your instinct
is truly an art."

23

Bug smiled gently
when he gave that advice,
Then he went on his way,
looking back once or twice.

25

Life can go up,
and then sometimes down.
But each time I'll smile
and try not to frown.

27

Now Bug ventured forward
with more certainty;
Ensuring the selection
was a better guarantee.

Now feeling assured
and keeping his head,
He proudly strode
down the path where it led.

29

Then Pumpkin showed up
and gave him a start,
and Bug felt his courage
begin to depart.

"I'm starting to worry
I'm not so astute;
I don't have a map,
so I don't know the route."

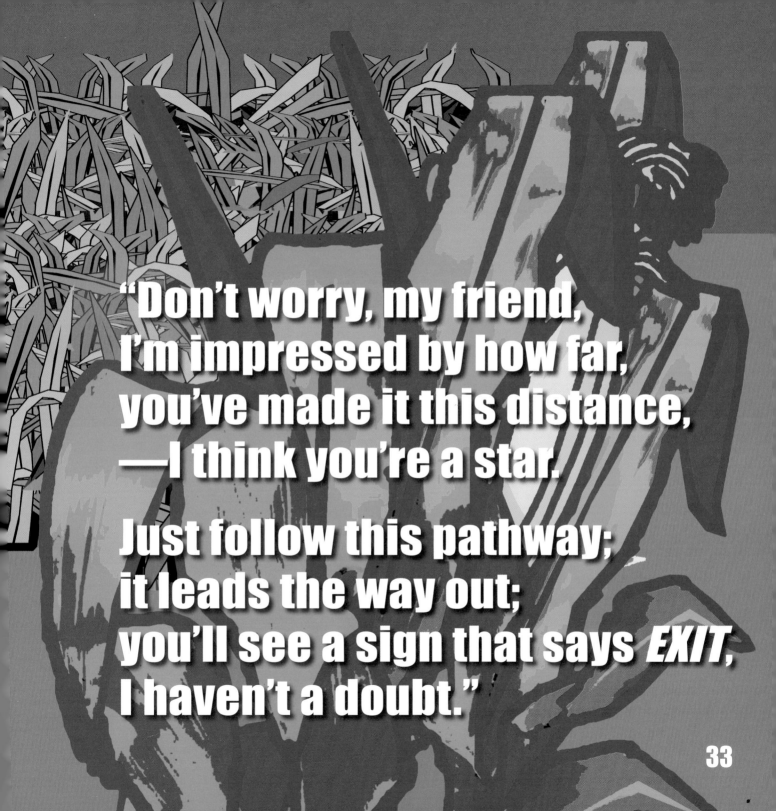

"Don't worry, my friend,
I'm impressed by how far,
you've made it this distance,
—I think you're a star.

Just follow this pathway;
it leads the way out;
you'll see a sign that says *EXIT*,
I haven't a doubt."

33

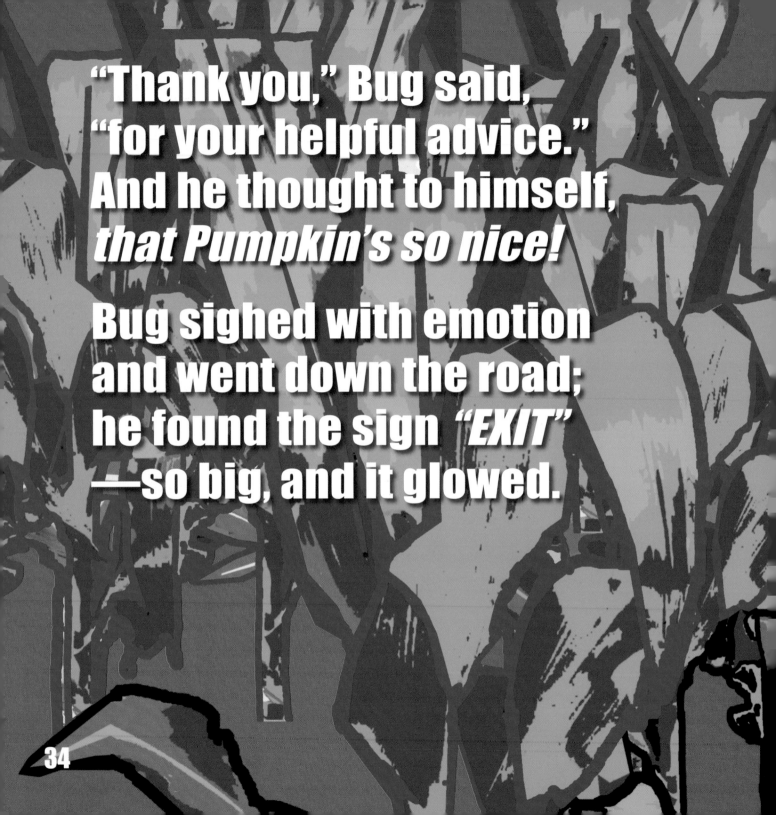

"Thank you," Bug said,
"for your helpful advice."
And he thought to himself,
that Pumpkin's so nice!

Bug sighed with emotion
and went down the road;
he found the sign *"EXIT"*
—so big, and it glowed.

Bug continued, assured,
and felt so impressed
with all that he'd learned;
it was all for the best.

He summed up his challenge
as he continued his ride:
*have confidence and faith
in what you decide.*

So get out the door
and try something new,
there's adventure out there,
merely waiting for you.

Even the smallest
stride that you make,
is the key to your future;
it will shake you awake.

39

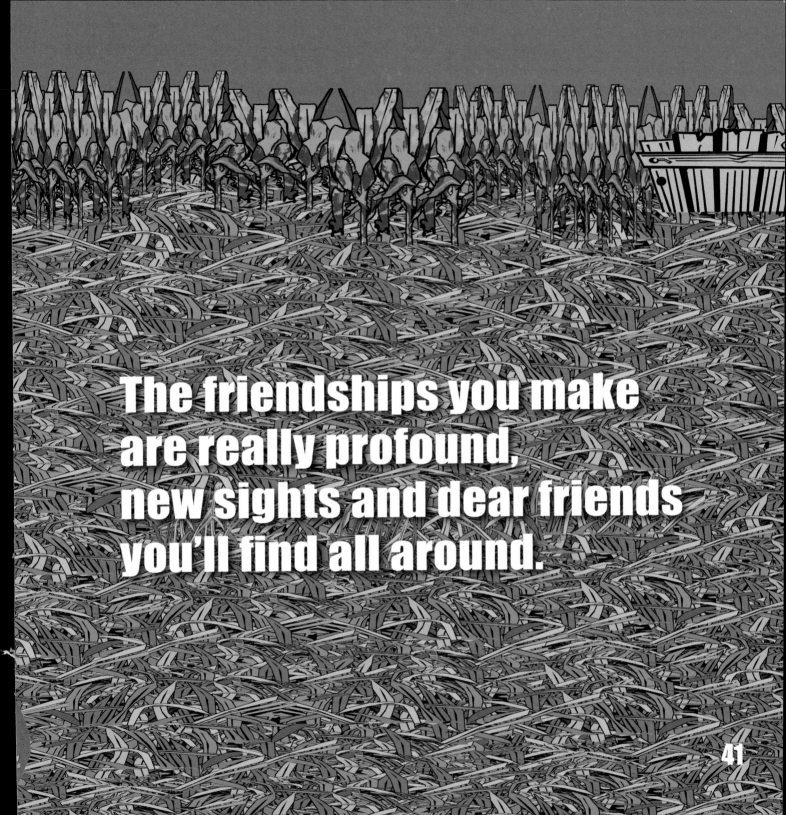

The friendships you make
are really profound,
new sights and dear friends
you'll find all around.

41

42

You may be surprised;
it's contagious, you know—
Taking a *chance* helps you
reach, stretch, and grow.